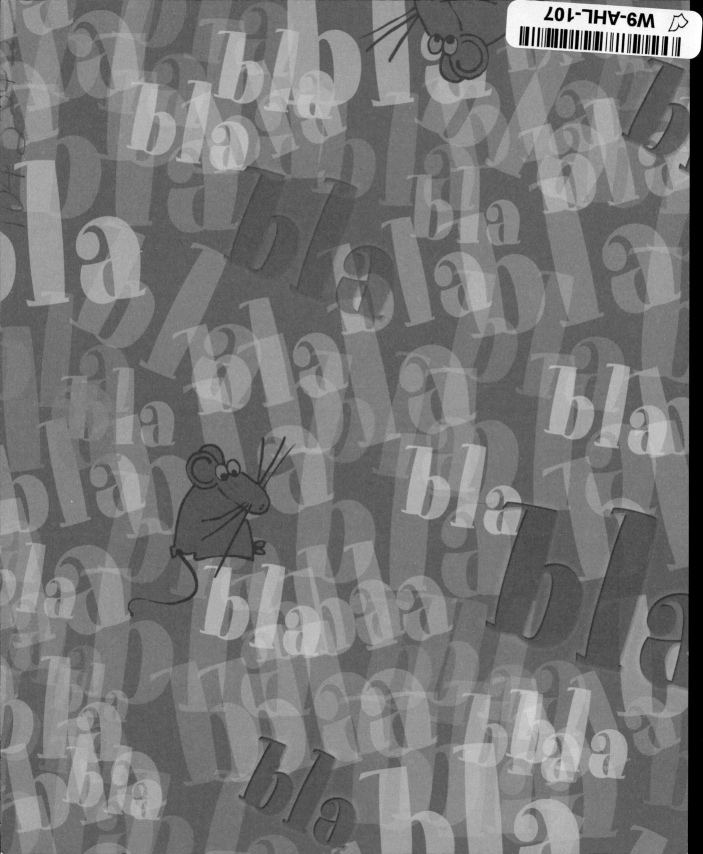

They say
he said
she said

nicanitas
BOOKS FOR CHILDREN

© Hardenville S.A.
Andes 1365, Esc. 310
Edificio Torre de la Independencia
Montevideo, Uruguay

ISBN 9974-7925-0-9

Printed in China

They say
he said
she said

Texts

Loti Scagliotti

Illustrations

Loti Scagliotti
Andrea Rodríguez Vidal

Design

www.janttiortiz.com

Translation

Jack Patrick Sullivan

They say this story began at the table
when Teresa told her son,
"Go and get Tom and tell him to come
and help us get rid of that mouse
running around in the house."

When John got to Tom's,
he learned that Tom was away,
and they say he said to Tom's sister Roxanne
that his mother had found
a mouse nibbling on an apple
in his house.

Without hesitation or interrogation, Tom's sister rushed out and screamed at the top of her lungs, "There's a mouse hidden in a corner of the house!"

And then, when Cristina
   -the neighbor nearby-heard her cry,
she told Patricia with a sigh,
"There's a mouse in our town
   that scares everyone around."

They say that Patricia said
            without malice to her aunt Alice,
"Aunt Alice, my dear, did you hear?
There was a single mouse
    in a house in town and now there is
            at least a mouse in every house.
It's MICE, my dear, and there's so much fear!"

Aunt Alice was desperate. She called the cops and they say she said that the mice had multiplied and everyone was petrified, and... who is it that did this, anyway?

The sergeant immediately gave the order, "Find the rascals! Search everywhere!"

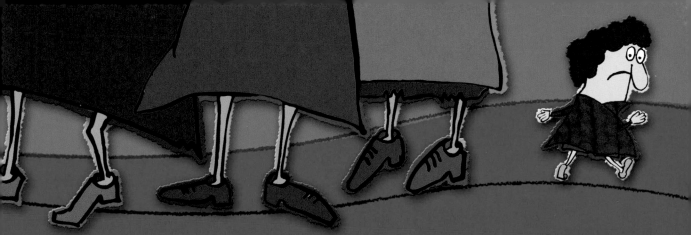

The lieutenant, obediently,
        ran out to interrogate.
He started with Jake who was in
        his garden using a rake.
"Did you see anything strange?"
                        he asked.
They say that Jake said
        with a nod of his head,
"There he goes, silently, swiftly,
        fleeing behind the crowd."

They say that Anita said to the lieutenant, "Catch him, he's running over the bridge and behind the crowd!"

But nevertheless, Julian reached for the thief,
slipped, missed and fell on his head,
barely touching the man, the scoundrel,
the rascal, the thief, who, they say, said

"I'm out of here! I must get away!"
And off he ran, all the way
to Teresa's house.

At Teresa's house, the police caught up to him at last. The angry crowd awaited him, chanting, "Punish him. Lock him up."

Looking at them, he bravely declared, "Dear friends, my name is Tom and I have come to get rid of the mouse in Teresa's house!"

Everyone was
really amused
from being so confused
that they laughed and they
smiled in celebration.
There was no price to pay
for all that had happened that day.
No mice, no mouse. No rascals, no thief
Although... it is said that there was a
letter, a love letter no less,
that arrived addressed
to the mouse in Teresa's house.

"WHAT DID THEY SAY? WHAT DID HE SAY?" COLLECTION

THEY SAY HE SAID SHE SAID

This little story with its absurdness and humor has allowed me to get children to consider two problems. The first one is how fear comes exclusively from the mind and is far removed from true events. The second one deals with the difficulties that can result from interpreting information through successive re-tellings.

Often, events that alarm us have little to do with reality, instead they are born from the mind. How often have we experienced dramatic fears that never in fact came true? The feeling of apprehension and fear that is created by a confused mind is an anxiety I would like to allay in those children who read this story with their parents. Parents should reflect with their children on the harm that fear can cause in our ability to grow up.

Roxanne, Patricia, Cristina, Jake, the Sergeant and other characters are messengers with bits of information that become exaggerated and deformed in a play of mix-ups and subjective interpretations that uniquely affect each individual and his or her daily life. And what we learn as readers is that not all information is useful to us and much less necessary to define our lives.

LOTI SCAGLIOTTI

IT IS OUR HOPE THAT IN READING THESE STORIES, YOU AND THE CHILD NEXT TO YOU WILL SHARE A MOMENT OF LOVE.

MORE BOOKS, NEW TITLES AND OTHER LANGUAGES AT

WWW.NICANITAS.COM.AR